Of Love and Other Monsters

Conversation Pieces

A Small Paperback Series from Aqueduct Press

Subscriptions available: www.aqueductpress.com

About the Aqueduct Press Conversation Pieces Series

The feminist engaged with sf is passionately interested in challenging the way things are, passionately determined to understand how everything works. It is my constant sense of our feminist-sf present as a grand conversation that enables me to trace its existence into the past and from there see its trajectory extending into our future. A genealogy for feminist sf would not constitute a chart depicting direct lineages but would offer us an ever-shifting, fluid mosaic, the individual tiles of which we will probably only ever partially access. What could be more in the spirit of feminist sf than to conceptualize a genealogy that explicitly manifests our own communities across not only space but also time?

Aqueduct's small paperback series, Conversation Pieces, aims to both document and facilitate the "grand conversation." The Conversation Pieces series presents a wide variety of texts, including short fiction (which may not always be sf and may not necessarily even be feminist), essays, speeches, manifestoes, poetry, interviews, correspondence, and group discussions. Many of the texts are reprinted material, but some are new. The grand conversation reaches at least as far back as Mary Shelley and extends, in our speculations and visions, into the continually-created future. In Jonathan Goldberg's words, "To look forward to the history that will be, one must look at and retell the history that has been told." And that is what Conversation Pieces is all about.

L. Timmel Duchamp

Jonathan Goldberg, "The History That Will Be" in Louise Fradenburg and Carla Freccero, eds., *Premodern Sexualities* (New York and London: Routledge, 1996)

Published by Aqueduct Press
PO Box 95787
Seattle, WA 98145-2787
www.aqueductpress.com

ISBN: 978-1-933500-16-4
ISBN-10: 1-933500-16-6

Cover Design by Lynne Jensen Lampe
Book Design by Kathryn Wilham
Original Block Print of Mary Shelley by Justin Kempton:
www.writersmugs.com

Cover collage painting: *String Theory* by Pam Sanders

Cover photo of Pleiades Star Cluster
NASA Hubble Telescope Images, STScI-2004-20
http://hubble.nasa.gov/image-gallery/astronomy-images.html
Credit: NASA, ESA, and AURA/Caltech

Printed in the USA by Applied Digital Imaging, Bellingham, WA

Conversation Pieces
Volume 18

Of Love and Other Monsters

A Novella

by

Vandana Singh

For my non-Euclidean friends, especially L.R.

My body I shall make a lamp,
My blood the oil, my life the wick;
And in its light I will see
The face of my Love...

Indian Sufi poet Kabir (1389 – 1518 A.D.)

When I think about him I remember a wave I watched near a beach once, a big, beautiful, smooth wave, perfectly rounded, like molten glass. It came into a narrow channel from the open sea, muscular and purposeful, hardly breaking into surf. I thought it would climb all the way up the end of the channel, wash over me, and carry on, unbroken, till it crossed the entire Deccan peninsula. But it met the sand, rolled over it, little traceries of white disturbing its smooth, translucent aspect. Touched my toes, broke up into little tongues of froth, and dissipated. So I like to think of him—Sankaran, I mean—like a wave that came out of the ocean for a while to fulfill some purpose (whatever that was). Then he was lost to me.

Physicists have a name for that kind of wave. It is very unusual, and it is called a soliton, or solitary wave.

When, as a young man, I met Sankaran for the first time, I thought he was the one I had been searching for all my conscious life. But as the poet Faiz says, there are more sorrows in the world than love. As soon as

I had settled into a certain youthful complacency, the world and its attendant sorrows got in the way.

The study of minds, soliton-like or otherwise, is my particular passion. Mind-sensing, mind-weaving—these extraordinary abilities set me apart from other people. I like to go into a gaggle of housewives bargaining over turnips or a crowd at a cricket match. I drift about, trying to determine what kind of entity the crowd has the potential to become. I take the embryological possibility of the meta-mind, make a joining here, a parting there; I wave my baton like the conductor of an orchestra and sense a structure, a form, coalesce in the interactions of these knots of persons. The meta-mind I construct has a vague unity of purpose, a jumble of contradictory notions, and even a primitive self-awareness.

Which is why I am so disturbed by solitons. They walk into a meta-mind as though nothing were there, and they walk out, unaffected. They give nothing, nor do they take away.

Such was Sankaran-with-stars-in-his-eyes, Sankaran the astronomer. This is not his story, however—his is just one thread in the tapestry, one voice in the telling. This is my story, and it begins when I was (so I am told) seventeen years old.

The first thing I remember is fire. The next thing: a pair of big, strong hands stroking and kneading me. A woman's voice, saying "Come now, be so, be still…" I was lying on a bed of warm ash, with sharp bits digging into my back.

I have no recollection of my life before the conflagration took my memory and identity. What I am now began with fire, with a woman called Janani, on a summer night in the remote outskirts of a small town in Eastern India. Later, when I came to my senses the stars were out, and the air smelled of roasted coriander seeds and cow dung, as it does most nights over there. I was lying on a cot in the little yard behind Janani's shack. Everything, including my lean, dark body, was unfamiliar to me.

My rescuer, Janani—a widow who ran a toddy shop—took me in and helped me face my predicament. The first thing she did after I recovered was to give me a name: Arun, which (like everything in those early days) sounded strange to me. "It means 'red,'" she told me. "You were born of fire." In those days I could sense the ghost of my past self very faintly: I saw symbols, words, numbers, shapes, as though scratched in damp clay. "Who am I? What happened to me in the fire?" I asked her. My voice sounded rasping and unfamiliar. The Hindi syllables felt strange on my tongue, but the words were there in my mind, waiting for me.

"I cannot tell you," she said. "There was a fire in an abandoned building, and I rescued you. You are not a local. That's all there is to know."

Without an identity I had nowhere to go, no family. Nobody in the area recognized me. So Janani gave me a home. I slept in the front of her hut, which was the toddy shop. Oh, the strangeness of those days!

It was like learning to live again. She had to show me how to take a twig from the neem tree behind the hut and use it like a toothbrush. I learned how to use a toilet, how to chop onions, how to talk to customers. Janani made a living not just from selling toddy but also by dispensing herbs for ailments from stomach aches to unrequited love, and I had to learn the lore enough to know which bottle to bring out when she asked for it. I had to learn to recognize my own face in the mirror—I would stand before the little mirror on the wall and pull faces until she yelled at me: "Arun, you fool! Did I pull you out of the fire so you could admire your beauty all day?" And she would set me to work washing glasses or chopping herbs. The ghost of my past self stayed in the shadows of my mind, and I found myself thinking less and less of what my old life might have been. At that time all was new, strange, and endlessly fascinating—not least of which was my ability to sense minds.

I was idle by nature and by the nature of my ability, which was distracting to say the least. Janani insisted on educating me; from her I learned my letters and arithmetic, which seemed to come very easily to me. She also got a retired clerk who frequented the tea-shack nearby to teach me a little about history, geography, and the rudiments of the English language. I would have liked nothing better than to loiter all day in the marketplace, but Janani's sharp tongue kept me at my chores and lessons, at least until her back was turned. She was stocky and strong; she moved with the cadence of a large, slow river, sweeping up everything in her path. Her customers, work-worn laborers and ne'er-do-wells, feared her and confided their woes to her. Only once did I see her take a man into the dark room behind the shop where she slept. After several hours he came out, staggering, smiled vaguely at me, handed me a ten-rupee note, and left. He never came back.

My favorite place, where I learned and practiced what I considered to be my art, was the market; here the vendors squatted on the ground before their baskets full of gourds, peppers, eggplants, and onions, shouting, "Rob me! Loot me! Only three rupees a kilo!" I grew to appreciate the sweaty housewives with their glinting eyes, their bright sarees hitched up in readiness for battle as they began insulting the produce. Pride, honor, and desire amidst the tottering, shining piles of luscious fruits and vegetables—how could I resist? I sensed the convoluted topography of each mind, its hills, valleys, areas of light and darkness, the whole animal mass trembling and shifting with emotional fluxes. After some practice I was able to draw the minds into a kind of net, to weave the separate threads of jangling thought-processes into—not a tapestry, I was never that skilled—but a jumble of knitting wool, such as a kitten might do. There was little awareness among the separate minds that they were, at this point in space and time, tentatively the members of a rather confused meta-mind—how many cells in your body, but for a specialized few, are aware of themselves as part of a higher consciousness?

I once tried to draw Janani into a meta-mind with a couple of her customers, but she came into the back of her shop and cuffed me. "Don't you try that on me, you good-for-nothing! Is this how you repay me?" I had already guessed (from the fact that nobody had tried it on me and that my subjects seemed to be so unaware of what I was doing) that this ability of mine was unique, but I didn't know that Janani knew I had it. Later she explained that she did not possess my ability—indeed, she had come across only one other person who did—but she was a sensitive. She could tell when someone, especially a crude beginner like me, was trying tricks.

"Who's this other person?" I asked, intrigued.

"You don't need to know anything about him," she told me. "Just somebody I met once. He wasn't a nice man."

She wouldn't tell me more. But I realized then that the world was more complex than I'd thought; at least one other person had my peculiar talent, most didn't, and some could sense my mind reaching out to theirs.

I spent all my spare time wandering about the narrow green lanes of my neighborhood under the gulmohar trees, scuffing up soft, silken dust with my bare toes. In the muddy by-lanes I gambled at marbles with other boys and gawked with them over the calendar of dewy-eyed film stars hanging in the neighborhood tea shack. I learned about sex and desire by watching the pariah dogs in the streets and the way the older boys looked at the unreachable, uniformed schoolgirls passing by with pigtails swinging. My own longings were nebulous. I could look at the tea-seller's daughter—a sloe-eyed vixen with a sharp tongue and a ready vocabulary of swear words—and tell that underneath it all was a mind as fragile as a spider's web, tense with fear and need. I felt drawn to her, but then there was also the barber, a thin, clean-shaven young fellow, shy and subdued to all appearances. He distracted me every time I passed the place where he had set up shop: a mirror hung on a wall by the street with a chair in front of it, where he sat his customers down and ministered to their heads or beards. His mind was luscious, imaginative, erotic; I could not read his thoughts, but I could sense the nature of them: desire flowed with the rise and fall of his fingers, the shy caress of his hands on the cheek of a customer. Both my mind and body responded to the needs of such men and women around me; sometimes I would get aroused simply walking down the street, feeling the brush of their minds like feathers on my skin. Due to the crowded, public nature of our lives and the narrowness of convention, there was little hope of physical consummation—only the occasional groping in dark alleyways among us boys—but I could reach out with my mind and make a bridge, a connection as tangible to me as a touch. Most did not have the ability to sense this, but once the tea-seller's daughter looked up at me, startled, her eyes as clear and honest as a small child's, as though she too had felt the electricity between our minds. Then her habitual aloofness slipped over her face like a mask, and the moment was gone.

There was a game I liked to play: I would lie on the broad branch of a large neem tree that grew near the tea-shop, close my eyes, and try to guess who was passing below me from their mind-signature. If the person was a stranger, the mind-signature told me nothing of their identity, not even if they were male or female—

but a well-known person was like the familiar topography of the street you grew up on.

Despite my persistent questions Janani refused to tell me about the other person she knew who had my ability. "I hope you never meet him," she would say with a shudder.

Then one night he found me.

I had just finished sweeping out the shop, when I sensed something odd, as though a tendril had insinuated itself into my mind; at the same time I became aware that there was someone outside the door, just standing and waiting in the darkness. Janani must have felt it too, because she looked at me in sudden apprehension. I felt the tug of a mind far more sophisticated than my own, pulling me into the labyrinths of its own consciousness like a fisherman drawing in his line. I got up and began walking toward the front of the shop as if in a dream. Janani, who was obviously less affected than I, grabbed me and pushed me out the back door, into the quiet darkness of her vegetable garden. "Arun, you fool, get out of here!" she whispered fiercely against my cheek. I willed myself to put one foot before another. I climbed across the bamboo fence. Every step I took made me stronger and more able to resist.

When I returned, Janani was sitting on the shop floor, rocking to and fro. Her hair was unkempt, her sari crumpled, and she kept saying "Rama, oh Rama," in a soft monotone. A great wave of anger and fear swept over me.

"Who was that? What did he do?"

"That was Rahul Moghe. The only other person I know who has your talent. He is dangerous, and he wants you, God knows for what terrible purpose. You must avoid him. You will know him not by his appearance, which can be deceptive, but by the way he drags at your mind without warning.

"He has threatened me. Now this place is no longer safe for either of us. I must think what to do…"

That was the first and only time Janani took me to her bed, to the comfort of her dark, Himalayan breasts that smelled of cloves and cinnamon. She was like an earthquake and a tidal wave rolled into one. Afterwards, I heard her mutter to herself: "surely it doesn't matter with him, he's different…" In the morning she flung me summarily out of her bed and began to pack.

"This is a sign that we must part ways. I have taught you what I can. You will go out into the world and make something of yourself, and keep away from Moghe. I have some money I have been saving for you. Meanwhile I will sell this place and go live with a friend in Rishikesh. Keep in touch with me, because I want to know how you are faring. I have some of your things in a safe place. I will send them to you when I can."

"What things?"

"Things from before the fire. Don't worry about it now. You must go to the next town and get a job. I know a place…"

Which is how I found myself living in a tiny room over a tailor's shop in the neighboring town. It was a tranquil time for me. I helped the tailor with deliveries, and after a while he made me a pair of pants and a shirt so I could look like a respectable young man instead of

9

a drifter with holes in his clothes. Eventually (prompted by a barrage of letters from Janani) I got a job as a clerk at a computer training institute. Here my quick brain and my lessons with Janani and the old clerk paid off; over the next year I improved my English and began to help the system administrator with computer maintenance work. The work was enjoyable and came to me easily.

"Arun, foolish one," Janani wrote. "You are no longer a street waif with few prospects. Here is your chance to make something of yourself. I'm sending money for classes. Learn computers and get a proper job; every idiot is doing it." So I registered for a couple of classes and found that I had a knack for programming. Numbers, symbols, instructions, logic—it was as though I had once known this or something like this, in my old life. Encouraged by the students, who looked upon me as a project of their own, I began to study full-time. Although I had no formal education and was unused to discipline, I made progress with their help. In the hot, dusty little classrooms with the squeaky ceiling fans and traffic sounds from the open windows, I was able to shut out other minds and concentrate. Slowly I began to write, decipher, and debug computer code. In a few months other students were asking me for help. My life changed.

Back in my bare little room I would lie on my sagging bed and listen to the voices from the shop below, the lulling rhythm of the sewing machines, and play at making meta-minds. "Arun," I would tell myself. "In two years you've come a long way." But my laziness, held at bay by the unaccustomed intellectual stimulation, reasserted itself eventually. Instead of pursuing a full degree I opted for a mere diploma, which greatly disappointed Janani as well as some of my teachers.

But the change in my life, in this short, intense period, had opened me up to the possibilities of the world. I read voraciously in Hindi and English, learning about foreign countries and customs, and the wars and plagues of history. From lurid Hindi science fiction to paperback English romances, there was nothing that was not grist for my mill. I came to realize that sensing other minds through the written word was almost as interesting a skill as my unique, innate ability to sense them directly. Writing—whether English or Hindi or computer code—was the key that opened the doors to other minds, other lands. Like a monk on leave from the monastery, I was agape with wonder. For the first time I realized that there were many ways to be a foreigner; losing one's memory, being poor, being illiterate, were just some of them.

Meanwhile I continued to get letters and packages from Janani. She was now a seamstress in Rishikesh. She wrote that she was gradually retrieving and returning my things, such as they were, from before the fire. The things made no sense. There were some photographs that she had apparently taken herself: a great, dazzling wall of flame, an enormous log in the foreground, glowing with the heat. Pieces of abstract ceramic sculpture, remains of etchings. Had I been an artist? There was nothing remotely artistic about me now. I looked at my hands, my body, clean and healed by Janani's ministrations. I did not even have any scars. I looked at the other photos she had sent of teenage boys looking into the camera. One of them was me. The others looked vaguely familiar. Had they been my friends in that unknown life?

But I was too busy with my new life to pay much attention to my erstwhile possessions. Not long after receiving my diploma, I got a job checking software for defects and moved to the great, crowded metropolis of New Delhi. Janani was ecstatic. "A great step up in the world, Arun!" she wrote, exulting. And in many ways it was so. Flush with success—the job was easy for me and not too demanding—and with a new sense of my place in the world, I settled down in my new life. It was during this time that I began to explore my extraordinary mental abilities in a more methodical manner.

One of my early discoveries was that there were minds that were completely closed to me, different from the kind of mental resistance I'd felt with Janani. There were people who would be standing with the crowd outside the cricket stadium, apparently as excited about the impending match as anybody else, but they did not register on my radar. I was greatly troubled by such minds—blanks, I called them. I feared and distrusted them. It seemed that my skill had its limitations. But the solitons were different. I sensed them, all right, but I could not draw them in. Their minds moved through my jumbled meta-mind the way a man walks through a large, empty field on his way home. Quickly, cleanly, with his attention elsewhere. Taking nothing, leaving nothing behind.

The first one I experienced was at a rally at the Red Fort in Delhi. The prime minister was up on the ramparts in a bullet-proof box, speechifying about the latest war. Seventeen thousand people with nothing better to do—college students, farmers with harvests lost in the drought, clerks on their way to important errands, unemployable sons of rich men and other wastrels, street people and pickpockets—had been rounded up by the party men. As the prime minister's rhetoric became more passionate, I sensed the minds, at first relaxed and disjointed like a bunch of loose rubberbands, becoming like angry bees buzzing in concert. Not very interesting—too simple, but also dangerous. I put my hands over my ears, but I could not shut them out; it was as though I were being blinded and deafened at the same time. Stumbling away through the crowd, I was pushed and cursed as I pressed on. And the realization hit: the meta-mind had formed of its own accord. I had not done it. That is why I couldn't make it stop. What such a self-generating meta-beast could do, who knew? The crowd surged around me, thrusting and clawing at me. I imagined the monster going out into the streets, maiming and killing, crying for blood. As my own mind dissolved into chaos, something strange and wonderful happened. I sensed a deep and momentary stilling in my mind, as though I had crossed a great, noisy battlefield into a waterfall of peace. Just for one glorious moment. Then the bees hummed in my head again, and it was all I could do to stagger about like a drunk at the fringes of the crowd, looking for that person. Useless, of course. Who walked so cleanly through the mad tangle that was the meta-beast, like a monk striding serenely through the sinful glitter of the world?

I learned later that there are only a few people like Sankaran, and that for very brief periods of time, all people are like that. But some sustain that state of mind for most of their waking life. A cobbler mending shoes in front of a cinema hall in Mumbai. A mathematician walking, seeing not the world but equations and things. A mother, single-minded about her ailing son. A lover in a dusty old garden, oblivious to roses. Yes, later I understood this state of mind.

Life in the big city was never boring. There was scope for my abilities, and they led me into unexpected adventures. One time, while strolling through the fort city of Old Delhi, I came upon a young girl standing in a doorway. She was a waif, barely in her teens, incongruously dressed in a bright red salwaar kameez that was too big for her. The narrow street was full of people and noise, bicycle bells and the calls of fruit sellers, and the light had the dazzling clarity of high summer. Seeing her in the dark archway of an old building with the sunlight washing her thin face, I felt the anguish of her mind like a blow between the eyes. I sensed a hopelessness so absolute that instinctively I moved toward her. She drew back from me, and a man appeared out of the shabby darkness of what I then realized was a brothel.

That was how I met Dulari. My rescue of her involved most of my meager savings (her price) and a local women's group. She was eventually given a job at a clothing shop that employed dozens of emaciated young women to sew name-brand clothes for overseas markets. I went to see her occasionally, but most of the time, guilt made me stay away. Although her life was better than before, it was still no life for a fourteen-year-old girl. But I was now a member of the middle class. I had to pretend to a certain decorum. Besides, I lived in a tiny room sublet to me by a large and boisterous Punjabi family. Dulari had no place in my life.

But I could not hide from myself the fact that I could have loved her. She was a child, and it was not appropriate, but I saw past her painfully thin, broken body into her mind. She was like the proverbial lotus that grows in murky water; its roots are soiled, but it climbs upwards, bifurcating into petals that open to the sky. Under the scars, a part of her was untouched by the privations and humiliations of her life; there was intelligence, hope, and layers of wonderful complexity and potential that perhaps would never find expression.

My colleague Manek was another matter entirely. He was well educated, had prospects, and was earning a reasonable salary. His mind—I could never look upon a person as simply a corporeal entity—was clean and simple, like an orderly room, and his thoughts and emotions were often quite transparent. One day, I sensed that he was depressed and asked him about it. In his simple, direct way, he told me that he was in love with a young woman he could not marry. There were caste and class issues, and his beloved's family was keeping guard around the clock so the couple could no longer meet. To make matters worse, his parents were now looking for a suitable girl for him. Naturally I became Manek's confidant.

That summer my landlord and his family decided to go home to their village in Punjab for the holidays. They padlocked all the doors in the apartment except for my room, the kitchen, and the bathroom and left me to a peace and privacy I had never before enjoyed.

So Manek came to see me at home. One day he was near tears, and I put my arms around him to comfort him. After that we became lovers after a fashion. He was not gay, he said, but he wanted me to pretend to be a woman, to be held, caressed, and comforted. In his mind the illusion was so complete that as I lay with him, I could almost feel the swell of my breasts. Meanwhile I touched his mind with my own, furtively, tentatively. I think our occasional mental contact helped him relax, although he could not directly sense the tendrils of my mind. With his face buried against my bare shoulder he would whisper the names of all the women he had loved from afar, ending with Anjana, his beloved.

Later there was Sheela, a quiet mouse of a woman, the older unmarried daughter of a couple who lived in the flat above. Her sisters were married off; she was the plain one, apparently, so there was not much hope that she would find someone. In her love-making, as in her mind, she was bold, imaginative, and tender, but everything she said was by touch or glance. During our few assignations she never spoke a word. Once I broke our pact of silence by uttering the word *love*. She sat up on the bed, stared at me, her wide eyes filling with angry tears. "Don't you dare say that word ever again," she said fiercely. She leapt upon me and began to pull off my shirt. The dark places in her mind deepened, trembled, caves opened like mouths, rivers of emotion roared in the gorges, the hidden places of her soul. She was fascinating, but she did not want me. Ultimately, fate in the form of a divorced man looking for a wife took her away to some far city and another life.

Sometimes I worried about how different I was from other young men. I looked and dressed like a man, but I did not understand social conventions about what it meant to be a man or a woman. I could go out with other young men to seedy bars and drink beer, but I did not know that the women there were for flirting with, or that I should out-shout the other men in a bid to impress. I would sit down with a woman and ask her about her work, or about the embroidery on her blouse. Women colleagues found that when I was the only male present they could talk as easily about "women" things as if they were by themselves; once I took part in a discussion about their periods, even though my role was only that of interested questioner. "God, Arun, you're too much," they would say, suddenly remembering I was a man. I watched cooking shows with as much curiosity as cricket and wrestling. My ability to sense minds enabled me to see human beings as entities beyond man-woman categories. I decided, after some months of informal study, that rather than two sexes there were at least thirty-four. Perhaps "sex" or "gender" isn't right—perhaps a geographical term would be more appropriate—thirty-four climactic zones of the human mind!

But my peculiarities occasionally made me wonder about my future. My colleagues were falling in love, getting engaged, getting married. To me, each job was like a temporary resting place before the next thing, as was each relationship. Would my restlessness be my undoing? Janani dismissed my fears. "You are young," she wrote in a letter. "Learn about the world, Arun. Embrace it. Love as many people as you can, but don't let anyone keep you like a bird in a cage."

By the time I met Sankaran I had learned a lot. Never to go to political rallies, for one thing. Or religious processions, although temples, churches, gurudwaras, and mosques were all right in small doses. I had also learned that contrary to what you might expect, families do not generally make good meta-minds. There is too much pushing and shoving about. They coalesce and come apart. Maybe they maintain a dynamic rather than a static equilibrium, because they are, after all, with each other day in and day out. Perhaps a meta-mind, indefinitely sustained, eventually goes mad.

I also did some experimenting with animals. There was a herd of cows that foraged in the street outside my apartment complex. They stood in the midst of traffic like humped, white islands, peacefully chewing cud, or waited with bovine patience for people to dump their kitchen refuse at the corner garbage dump. I sensed their minds but did not always understand the nature of their thoughts. One night, returning from work, I saw a magnificent bull standing in the middle of the road, on the median. Traffic swept by him on either side. In the luminous dust under the streetlamps, he was like a great white ghost. Across the road the cows lay regarding him with indifference. I sensed his mind as clearly as if it had been visible. He was calling to the cows with all he had, a long, soundless low of desire. The cows' response was, in effect, *not today, pal, we have cud to chew.* It was then that I realized that animals could not only sense each other's minds, but also communicate mentally.

I continued my experiments with human minds, learning all kinds of interesting trivia. For instance, odd numbers, especially primes, make more stable meta-beasts; even numbers are less steady, especially if there are only two people involved. Couples are really dangerous, because there is nothing to balance the connection between the minds, no push to counter the pull, if you know what I mean. Which is why, long before I met Sankaran, I had decided never to fall in love.

I met him in America. Janani encouraged me to go there after she heard from a fellow sensitive that Rahul Moghe had been seen in Chandigarh, only a few hours drive from Delhi. I felt the old, nameless fear again. I had not thought about Rahul Moghe in years. At that time my company was exporting a team of software people to the United States. Urged by a fury of letters from Janani, I joined the exodus to the land of milk and honey.

In America's small towns, with their abnormally clean streets so strangely empty of people and animals, in the surreal, neon-bright canyons of vast, sky-scrapered cities, I found that I could further explore my ability to make meta-minds. Despite the much touted individualism of Americans, I often encountered large groups of people with similar belief systems and mental processes. In the beginning it was vastly entertaining; I walked down Wall Street, peered in at the Stock Exchange. All those people, thinking themselves competitors and rivals, muttering into cell phones and shouting like deranged children—what a seamless, stable meta-mind they made! Then there was suburban America, yuppie-ville, with the over-large houses and multiple cars and boats, where it was just too easy. Teenagers expressing their individuality in their name-brand clothing and angst-ridden looks were easy too, but there was a dark undercurrent in that meta-mind that disturbed me, hinting of dams upstream about to burst. I amused myself making meta-minds out of warring groups of political opponents and fundamentalist religious types with opposing loyalties. My own community of Indians, with few exceptions, lived in a time-warp, adopting conventions and practices that no longer existed in India. Their constant obsession with their status as high-earning professionals was boring. Far more interesting were splinter groups living on the edge of mainstream culture; I made friends with Wiccans, Mexican immigrants, and an Ethiopian gay couple that ran a restaurant in San Francisco. I lived in California at first, working as little as I could get by with, indulging my special ability to the hilt. Despite all this I felt a deep and increasing loneliness at the back of my mind, a longing not just for my old haunts in India, for old friends and people I had known, but for something beyond that. Already I was making a shape, a place for Sankaran inside me.

Then something happened that drove me from California. One bright Saturday morning I was swimming about in the shallows near a beach when I felt an undertow. I began to struggle against it; then I realized that it was in my mind. A powerful tug, reeling me in as though I were an exhausted fish. I recognized the summons that would not be denied. Rahul Moghe had found me at last.

I emerged from the water and found myself compelled to walk between sunbathers and colorful beach umbrellas toward a car parked on the road above the beach. I tried to stop, or to ask for help, but I was as helpless as a mannequin. As I came near the road one part of my mind noted that the car was a white sedan with tinted windows. A man in sunglasses sat in the driver's seat. He leaned forward to open the passenger side door. I remember that a gold ring flashed on his hand.

There was a sudden squeal of brakes, a shuddering crash. A bus, pulling into its stop just behind the car, hadn't slowed down enough. It rear-ended the parked car, buckling the back and making it rock forward. The pull of Rahul Moghe's mind ceased abruptly.

I took the chance; I ran to where my beach bag lay, picked it up, crossed the road out of sight of the accident, and sprinted furiously through the parking lot on the other side of the road. My bare feet burned on the concrete, but in a minute or two I was in my car, driving off to safety. A police car came in from the other direction, sirens wailing.

About twenty minutes later I felt Rahul Moghe's mind reach for me again, but his touch was faint, searching, tentative; a few minutes later I couldn't feel him at all.

Through sheer luck I had gotten away again.

I changed jobs, fled the West coast, and kept to old, sprawling Eastern metropolises like New York and Boston. Nearly a year passed. There was no sign of Rahul Moghe. Janani's letters also did not mention him except to warn me to be vigilant. She hoped I had seen the last of him.

I knew, however, that he would be back, that he would find me. I sensed this in a way that I did not understand. I would dream of him sometimes, of the long arms of his mind reaching for me, drawing me to him, to the abyss of his soul. He terrified me. But there was a part of me that wanted to know him, perhaps the only other person with my ability.

Then one afternoon, in a café in Boston, where I was attempting to drink what Americans fondly believe to be chai, I met Sankaran.

I was amusing myself constructing a meta-beast from the very uppity literary crowd in one corner and a dysfunctional family of four at the next table, when someone coasted through the whole mess of mental cobwebbing like it wasn't there. Instinctively I looked towards him. He was unmistakably Indian, delicately built, with a thatch of unkempt black hair and an apologetic and neglected mustache. His hands were slender and brown. He sat down with a book and a coffee cup and was soon lost in whatever he was reading.

I went across to him, trying to control my excitement. His being Indian provided an easy excuse to introduce myself.

He was a post-doctoral researcher at one of the universities scattered about this great city. He lived in a hole in Cambridge. While traveling on a bus he had gotten so engrossed in a collection of conference reports that he had gotten off at the wrong stop. Finding himself near a café, he had dropped in for a coffee and a good, long read.

"You mean you don't know where you are?"

He turned his brown eyes to me and smiled. For a moment he really seemed to be there in the café.

"Does any body?" he said, separating the "body" from the "any" with the precision of a surgeon. I thought this a deeply philosophical statement until he explained that he meant that since the earth and the solar system and the entire galaxy were constantly changing their places in space, one had to be very specific about reference frames. I was utterly charmed.

After I helped Sankaran find his way home, we became friends. He never sought me out, but I began to haunt a coffee shop in Cambridge where he turned up nearly every evening like a homing pigeon, armed with books and papers. When aware of the mundane world, he treated it with a bemused, indiscriminate kindness—being the kind of person who, upon bumping into people, doors, or potted plants, apologizes to them with equal courtesy. Much of the time I watched him over my coffee cup, filled with silent wonder. I could explore his mind, embrace it with my own, but I could not draw it to me, play with it, or manipulate it. He was untouched by my mental explorations. He had no need of me; he posed no threat. He filled the emptiness that had been growing in me.

I discovered in Sankaran some of the things that had drawn me to Dulari—but without the pain. His mind had the delicacy of petals about to unfurl and the innocence and wonder of a child beholding a rainbow for the first time. Instead of the white noise of contradictory emotions, the cacophony of thwarted desire and loneliness that make up a typical human mind, his mind possessed the deep peacefulness found in high places, in the thin air of Himalayan country above the snowline. He did not torture himself with questions about his purpose in life or what other people thought about him—indeed, the obsession with self was quite absent in him. He was beautiful; a being absorbed at play in a universe far vaster than ordinary humans could imagine.

Looking at him, at his thin, mahogany-brown body draped without grace on the sofa while his mind saw wonders I could only guess at, I was filled with the sweetness of desire. I wanted to touch his body as well as his mind. I wanted his touch, even if it were only as brief and innocent as a hand on my arm. In India, where platonic friends of the same sex often hold hands or fling arms around each other in public without censure or misunderstanding, it would have been easy. But social mores were different here, and—more to the point—he remained unaware of my need of him.

I spent as much time as I could with Sankaran. Sometimes I would meet him in the Physics department and amuse myself looking at star charts on the computer as he finished a colloquium or worked out his equations. He would join me at the computer when he was done and fill me with astronomical lore as we roamed the galaxy. Here was a red giant, there a supernova, a binary star system, a neutron star, a black hole, an extra-solar planet 15 times the mass of Jupiter. I learned the lexicon of astronomy as a lover learns the body of his love.

Gradually I got to know a little about Sankaran's background. He was from a learned Tamilian family. He was very fond of his mother and his elder brother, who remained in the ancestral home in Chennai after his father's death. I had a mental picture of the faded whitewash on the walls, the banana trees in the courtyard at the back. When he talked about his family, he seemed suddenly to come to earth.

"My mother's cooking, nothing like it." Or, "Unna taught me calculus in eighth class."

"They want for me to get married," he told me once, shyly. He shook his head. "I do not have time for a wife. But it is also tradition to continue your line. Life is not simple." He sighed. But for an accident of gender and the cruelty of convention, I would have married him in a minute.

He was also a devotee of Lord Shiva. He kept a small stone Shiva-lingam in his room, a shrine in a bookshelf surrounded by books and papers on astrophysics. There was only one picture on the wall—a photograph of the beautiful and graceful Tamilian actress Shobhana. Sankaran confessed shyly to me that he was a fan.

I feigned an interest in cooking so I could spend more time with him in the privacy of his room. As I stirred eggplant curry on the stove, I would look at him as he lay on the bed, flipping through the latest *Astrophysical Journal*, his eyes dreamy. He would mutter phrases that were meaningless to me, things like "virial theorem" or "off-main-sequence star." Sometimes I would ask him to explain, and I would perch on the bed next to him, feeling the heat of his body, the passion of his intellect. I would glance up at the stone phallus of Shiva and remember how it felt to pretend to be a woman for my old lover, Manek. In the little studio apartment the air would fill with the smell of roasting spices, cumin and coriander, and the sharp, enticing aroma of ginger. I would lean close to Sankaran, looking with him at incomprehensible pages of equations and star charts, conscious only of his nearness, the soft black hairs on his arms stirring in unison with the rhythm of his breath. I would stretch my mind toward his, enclosing him, burying myself between the flanks of his beautiful, oblivious mind. Sleepy with desire, I would remember that one of the manifestations of Shiva is Ardhanarishwaram: half man, half woman. Shiva is the one who dances the world into being and out of it. One day I said:

"Tell me something, Sankaran. If you could ask the Lord Shiva three questions, what would they be?"

He was silent for a while. Then he said,

"I would ask if the dark matter problem is truly a question of missing mass. Then I would ask about

26

the Higgs boson and the accelerating expansion rate. Which may be related to the very failure of the standard model I mentioned at the seminar. You have to consider…"

I would distract him gently back to my question. Each time I asked him the question, he would answer as though he had never been asked this before. One day, after he had read a letter from his mother, he sighed.

"I would like to ask Lord Shiva if there is some way I can avoid getting married without hurting my family."

And once:

"I would ask Lord Shiva if there is life on the extra-solar planets we have found. If there is life on other worlds at all."

I found myself falling into Sankaran's gravitational well as inevitably as a star being swallowed by a black hole.

Janani cautioned me not to focus on Sankaran to the exclusion of other things. "Explore your ability," she wrote. "Travel a bit. See the world, Arun. Immerse yourself in it. We think all we have are our paltry possessions and the special people in our lives. But the world is greater than that…"

Her advice came too late. I remember wondering about the tone of Janani's letter—she was not one to wax philosophical as a rule. It occurred to me that she never wrote about her life in Rishikesh, or the woman she worked with—I had never thought to ask about these things. But then I had a new distraction. Sankaran got a phone call from his elder brother in India. The family had found him a bride. He was to go home in a week to tie the knot.

27

He told me the news with a resigned air. Clearly he saw marriage as a duty to endure with good grace. We sat in silence for a while, my own mind reeling with dismay and resentment. Then Sankaran turned back to his notes and scribbled away at his equations, quite happily lost in his universe of stellar wonders, and I was relieved. The wife would be a nuisance, and I would have to find a way to spend time with Sankaran without her interfering, but she could never truly touch him, never own him. How could one woman compete with a trillion burning suns?

I saw him off at the airport. As I felt the quiet comfort of his mind recede, I staggered out into the warm light of a spring day, a man adrift in a sea of blathering minds, without an island in sight.

The days of his absence are still clear to me: the heat of my apartment, the monotony of the days at work, the stupefying predictability of the minds around me that produced an answering dullness in my own soul.

Then came a letter from Janani that worried and mystified me.

"I am going on a journey to Thailand," she wrote. "I, who have never been out of India! I am very excited to be traveling on a plane and seeing the world, just as you have done. At my age too! Still, it is not a pleasure trip. I am on an adventure, Arun, the culmination of a life's work. I don't know if I will emerge from it unscathed. Meanwhile I have just sent you a parcel containing the last of your things. When you understand who you are, Arun, I hope you will forgive me…"

There was no way to contact Janani for details. The little shop where she lived and worked as a seamstress did not have a phone. I debated going to India to see her. The thought was tempting. I had not been home in three years. Perhaps later I could go down to Chennai and see Sankaran. I began making inquiries at a travel agent's.

But Providence had other plans.

A few days before I was to pay for my ticket, I woke up in the throes of a nightmare. I sat up in bed in the half-light of dawn, looking around at the familiar chaos of my room, wiping my sweaty hands on the bed-clothes. The monster that had been there in my dream was still present, however. I sensed it—a meta-mind of great power. It seemed to be some distance away, a fact that puzzled me. Even the self-generated meta-mind I had encountered at the rally in Delhi had had a fair-ly short range. I remembered how it had buzzed and hummed in my ears, driving me close to madness. This was something like that, but quieter. It was engaged in some kind of play, like a child absorbed in a toy. Only, this play felt dangerous.

I could have walked away from it, but I felt a deep curiosity mingled with fear. Where was this meta-mind? What was taking up its attention so completely? How had such a powerful thing come into being?

I dressed hurriedly, flung myself into the car, and began to drive toward it.

When I was halfway to Boston (having driven about ten miles) I realized it was much further than I had thought. What could make its presence felt from so far away?

My apprehension mounted the closer I got to it. As I drove between the tall buildings of the city, with the sunlight flashing on tiers of window panes, reflecting in my eyes, I realized that the meta-mind was different from any I had encountered. The one at the Red Fort had been a hasty and temporary thing, powerful only because it was made up of seventeen thousand minds. This thing had fewer components and was more focused, like a laser beam.

I came to a stop before an old brick office building. Sirens wailed; as I leaped out of my car, police vehicles and ambulances drove up, disgorging men in uniform. A crowd had collected in front of the building, looking skyward with a mixture of apprehension and ghoulish anticipation. I squinted against the glare of the sun and saw a man standing on a window ledge some seven stories above the street. He teetered, looked behind him, and jumped.

He seemed to fall in slow motion, his arms flung up as though in surrender. About halfway down, his mind, which had been locked in a trance-like state, woke up to screaming terror. Too quickly, a red flower blossomed on the sidewalk, and a splinter of bone buried itself in a watching woman's arm. People screamed, moving back, stumbling over each other. Blood spattered their clothes. TV cameras zoomed in as policemen began to shout orders.

Then the next one fell. A woman, her skirts billowing up. She broke like a cracked egg on the sidewalk.

In the screaming and confusion I darted into an entrance I'd noticed further along the sidewalk.

I took an elevator to the seventh floor. The meta-mind was still quivering with satisfaction. It was composed of not more than twenty minds, twisted and knotted together, not randomly but with the intricacy, order, and beauty of an integrated circuit or a Persian carpet. It was beautiful and deadly, and I sensed its hunger as it felt around for its next victim.

I entered a corridor with plush blue carpeting and chrome and glass décor. The place was cold and smelled of fear. People stood silently in little knots, with wide, frightened eyes. A troop of policemen were trying to force open one of the double-doors in the hallway. A large woman in a red business suit was flailing her arms and crying hysterically, "Another one! There must be another one!"

I stood very still, concentrating, stilling my own fears. My mind felt like it was being run over by a convoy of trucks. I thought of Sankaran, took a deep breath, and concentrated on undoing the meta-mind. I slipped into the meta-mind the way a snake enters a marsh, without a ripple, and started to unravel it, thread by thread, mind by mind. The exquisite patterns and symmetries were the work of a master. As I took it apart I regretted having to destroy something so beautifully constructed.

It came loose as though it had been turned off with a switch. I took a breath of relief, and found that my knees were shaking. I trembled all over, and little rivers of sweat dribbled down my face. Untangling it had taken more out of me than I had realized.

I leaned against the wall for support, fighting panic. Meanwhile the hysterical woman had stopped shouting and was looking around her in bewilderment. Tears started running down her face. The double-doors that the police had been trying to force opened suddenly, and a man looked out. He seemed dazed. The policemen pushed him aside and ran into the room. Inside, people were getting up from a table, passing hands over their eyes, shaking their heads, as though they were coming out of a trance. Sunlight streamed through an open window; the glass lay smashed on the floor, like diamonds. One of the men at the table looked at the window, the policemen. "What happened?" he asked.

I walked with difficulty to the elevator; every few steps I had to stop to lean against the wall. People around me were shouting, crying, and rushing about, and nobody took any notice of me. As I stumbled into the elevator I realized that only one person could have constructed a meta-mind so powerful.

Now I recognized the familiar swift current of his mind drawing me toward him. I staggered out of the lobby and around the corner of the building to a blue station wagon. I saw the tinted windows, the flash of the gold ring as the door opened. I got into the passenger seat almost thankfully, collapsing in a heap.

Rahul Moghe took off his sunglasses, looked at me, and smiled. I had an impression of largeness, although physically he was not more than average in height and build. Seeing him in his entirety, body and mind, was like looking at a vast ship with the prow head-on. His eyes burned like forest fires in his dark face—his arms reached toward me, pulling me into the seat. I heard the click of the seat-belt.

Much later, when I came to, the first thing I saw was his face, leaning over me. We were in a dingy hotel room. I remember the hardness of the bed on which I lay, the sunlight making a pool of brightness on the green carpet. I closed my eyes, but he was still there in my mind.

The feelers of his mind held me close, with an intimacy that terrified me. He spoke.

"You are a coward, Arun. You run from the only person who is like you. Why?"

The fingers of his mind opened every door, every barrier in my mind. He entered my memories, my secret places, the unknown depths of my consciousness. He gathered me to him, and hot pincers of pain gripped my head.

"What you saw just now is only the beginning of what we can do together. You don't know who you are, or how long I have needed you. Together we will build meta-minds that will make this last one look like a child. Come, I will train you, tell you how to use your power. But first let me tell you who you are. At last…"

His mind relaxed its hold on mine as he began to caress me. I was so tired; I had struggled for so long. Now I could rest. I had never known what it was like to reach across the void between one person and another and find a hand held out to grasp your own…

I hit him with all the strength I had. I got him squarely on his throat; he rolled off the bed and fell gasping and gurgling to the ground. My mind pushed his away as I leaped off the bed. He lay on the ground, clutching his throat, rolling from side to side.

As my hands fumbled with the door knob, a searing pain tore through my head. He was sitting on the floor, rubbing his neck, concentrating. Against my will, I turned around and walked back to him and sat helplessly on the bed. The pain receded. He sat beside me, his arms pushing me down until his face was leaning over mine.

"You don't know who you are, Arun. That bitch Janani took your memories away from you. Did you know that? She took away what you were. If I could resurrect you, I would. But all I can do now is to share with you…"

My vision blanked. I dropped into darkness, into a silence in which my own screams kept echoing. Terrifying images came crowding out of the dark—demon-like visages and shapes that kept morphing from one monstrosity to another. I fell with them toward a pale circle of light that opened up below me like the mouth of a well. Then I lost consciousness.

When I came to, Rahul Moghe was holding me up against his shoulder, trying to spoon something into my mouth. I gagged as chicken soup went down my throat, then licked my cracked lips and tried to struggle out of his grasp. The room spun.

"Take it easy," he said. A dim lamp lit the room; I saw that night had already fallen. I felt weak and spent.

"It was too much for you, too fast," he told me, spooning more soup into my mouth. "I see that I have to work against a great deal of conditioning. So much damage has been done…"

He let me sleep after that, but throughout my incarceration I never truly regained consciousness. I experienced brief periods of wakeful clarity, but for the most part I was in a confused, dream-like state during which I could not distinguish between reality and the nightmares that plagued me. Held in Rahul Moghe's fierce grip, his face against mine, I thought I heard voices of people I had known. Once it seemed a woman lay by me, painfully thin; she nestled sensuously against my shoulder and spoke in Dulari's voice. Another time I felt Sankaran prop me up to a sitting position. I thought I was being rescued at last, but he was holding a star chart in his hands, pointing at it, saying something insistently. Old friends—the boys I had played with in my teenage years, Manek—walked through my consciousness like ghosts. Always, Rahul Moghe was there in my mind, muttering in my ear in Hindi, English, and languages I could not understand. "You belong to me," he would say, "you and I are one of a kind...both alien, both lost, both pretending to belong..." And again: "Alone, our powers are nothing. Together we can do things..." Sometimes his words would echo in my head like muffled drumbeats: "power to change...to change...to change..." or "she burned you...burned you..." He would alternately entreat and reprimand me. "You think you belong, Arun," I remember him muttering against my ear. "But you live in a dangerous place outside the boundaries humans create around themselves. Man-Woman. Mind-Body... If your so-called friends could see you as you are, they would hate and revile you. I am the only friend you have, my love. We owe our allegiance to a different star..."

I saw myself falling again towards a pale sun, surrounded by demon-like wraiths that stretched long fingers toward me. "This is who you are," Rahul Moghe whispered. His hands raked my bare chest. As I bit back a cry of pain, I perceived it—his mind, opening before me like sunrise on a new world. I saw the power, the beauty, the ruthlessness of him—the mountain ranges, the sheer cliffs, vast Escher-like vistas. He was letting me into his soul.

And I turned to him, reaching out exploring arms toward this stupendous geography. As we lay entwined, he changed beside me—his skin paled, then darkened, his hair changed colors like a kaleidoscope. Arms and breasts and thighs moved against my skin—I had a glimpse of a great, hungry creature, all orifices and phalluses—and as I joined with him, I could no longer tell body from mind. Then, just as our bizarre mating reached its climax, he tore into me, tasting and feeding, ripping and slicing.

When eons later I opened my eyes, I was weak but able to think. Rahul Moghe lay beside me, asleep, one arm flung over my chest. Afternoon light filtered through the green plastic curtains. My mind felt as though it had been shredded and trampled on. To my horror I saw that the covers over my chest were stained with blood. Warily I groped about in my mind for him, but he was gone. Slowly and carefully I put myself back together, like an injured animal licking its wounds.

Just then I saw the door open halfway. An olive-skinned woman stood there, holding a pile of clean sheets, her mouth open. She backed out and shut the door behind her. Had I dreamed her? And if not, why had I not felt her mind? Why had Rahul Moghe not stirred, not known she was there? It came to me that she was a blank, one of those whose minds were inaccessible to me. And to him, also, I realized.

I must have fallen into exhausted slumber because when I woke again, the room was dark and the phone was ringing. Moghe stirred beside me, cursed, and turned on the lamp. He grabbed the phone and spoke into it for a few minutes in Hindi. His mind was quivering with excitement.

"Another of our kind has been found," he told me. "You are too weak to travel with me. I must leave you for a few days. Do not think of betraying me. A man in the hotel who is my servant will look after you."

When I found my voice it was barely a whisper.

"Where…?"

"Bangkok," he said. I fell asleep again and woke some time later to find a strange, dark-haired older man in the room, dressed in the hotel livery of white and green. His mind was like a cowering animal. "This is Odylio," Moghe said. He will feed you and check on you. Perhaps without me you will recover faster." He leaned toward me, and for a moment I saw the mouths of the demons that plagued my sleep. "Wait for me, Arun," he whispered, and then he was gone.

That night Odylio fed me soup. He did not try to talk to me. I was too weak to play any tricks with his mind; besides which, I suspected that whatever Rahul Moghe had done to this man could not be reversed by my poor skill. In Moghe's absence my mind slowly cleared; I began to think of escape, although it seemed impossible. Perhaps the soup had some drug in it—

I was still unnaturally weak. I lay helpless, sensing the minds of people passing by outside the door, but I could not even cry out.

Then, next morning after breakfast, the olive-skinned cleaning woman opened the door. She was holding a pile of towels. She gave me a nervous look and began to back out. I raised my hand weakly from the bed. "Help me!" I croaked.

She came slowly into the room, her eyes wide. She looked at me and said something I could not understand. She set the towels down, picked up the phone, and began speaking breathlessly in what I realized must be Portuguese.

I had avoided and feared blanks all my life; the irony of being rescued by one was not lost on me. I was taken to hospital by the police; lying there with the IV in my arm, I closed my eyes to stop the tears of relief and gratitude and to remember the face of my deliverer.

The police did not believe my story. Although I did not think there was much point in telling them the truth—mere forces of law and order could hardly contain a person such as Rahul Moghe—I was too weak to invent something more plausible. The hotel receptionist had said very clearly that the person who had checked in and taken the key of Room 323 was a young white woman called Marie Grenier from Baton Rouge, Louisiana. Nobody knew anything about an Indian man.

I never found out what, if anything, the Brazilian maid told the police, or whether they had believed her.

That night, I sat up in my hospital bed and detached the IV from my arm. I found my clothes folded neatly at the foot of the bed, and changed into them with some difficulty. There were bandages on my chest that hurt every time I moved. I dragged myself from corridor to corridor under garish fluorescent lights, choking on the antiseptic smell, until I came upon a side exit.

The cool night air revived my senses. With the last of my strength I found the nearest subway station, took a train journey that I can no longer remember, and went home to my apartment. I didn't have any of my things with me—I had to find the manager, who was not amused at being woken at four in the morning. I fell onto my bed and slept until noon.

When I woke my mind was mercifully my own. I was bruised and injured physically and mentally from my ordeal—I thought longingly of Sankaran's healing presence—but at the same time I dared to hope that I would recover.

I resigned from my job, telling my colleagues I had found work in Florida. I withdrew my savings from my bank and rented a room in a ramshackle apartment complex in Cambridge. I requested an unlisted phone number and obtained a post office box under a different name.

If it had not been for Sankaran, I would have fled to the ends of the earth. I don't think Moghe understood that. I believe that my subterfuge paid off because he expected me to leave Boston, to run before him as I had done before. I would no longer run.

Within a few days, I found a job working with a medical company as a lowly computer technician. It paid enough to keep me alive, and to maintain my car. Now assured of a livelihood and a roof over my head, I could no longer avoid thinking about my ordeal with Rahul Moghe and what it implied about my past. Janani's last parcel, which had arrived the day before I moved to my new apartment, confirmed that I had not dreamed up the events in that hotel room. Beset by an apprehension that it would tell me more than I wanted to know, I had not opened it for some days. But now that my new life, such as it was, had begun and the immediate fear of Rahul Moghe was gone, I had no excuses. I opened it.

The parcel contained the usual junk that Janani had sent me over the years, bits of broken metal and shards of ceramic, some with drawings and etchings on them. There was also a letter.

I read it. I looked at the contents of the parcel that I had piled on the bed. I read the letter again. I remembered Rahul Moghe whispering impossible things into my ear.

Alien, alien, alien, he had said. You and I owe our allegiance to a different star.

I looked at the strange objects on the bed. Whether I wanted them to or not, they began to make sense. The ceramic pieces, burnt black on one side, red on the other. The strange etchings, the pointillist ones in particular, one of them showing me a pattern I had seen before, not only on Sankaran's computer but also in my fevered dreams: the constellation Sapt-Rishi as seen from Earth. Then the pictures Janani had taken, of the boys so like me—they were all me, I realized, at various stages of formation.

I could no longer avoid the truth of my origin. I sat on my bed, watching night fall, shadows moving out from the corners of the room to fill it with darkness. Headlight beams swept across the curtained window, and through the thin walls I could hear my neighbors having an argument about laundry.

I laughed hysterically. After a while I started to cough, so I got up, turned on the light, and got a drink of water. Looking out of the grimy window at the busy street in front of my apartment complex, I had an impulse to cry.

Instead I went to the local pub and drank myself stupid. I told the bartender I was an alien. He gave me a sad look from beneath long, dark eyelashes and went on polishing glasses. "You won't believe how many people tell me that," he said. This set me off laughing again, until I was weeping large tears onto the bar. I don't remember how I got home. I slept like a dead person until late the next afternoon.

When I woke I had a headache the size of Antarctica; I staggered into the shower with my clothes on. Under the cold water some of my reason returned. I stripped, looking down at my all-too-human body. I thought about the notion that Janani was as much my murderer as my progenitor. She had burned me, Moghe had said. I understood now that I was stuck with this body, this gender, because of that. Unlike him, I could no longer change form; nor could I tell friend from foe. "Damn them all, Moghe and Janani and all," I told myself.

I spent two days in this insane state, staring at the things on my bed, re-reading Janani's letter. Rahul

Moghe appeared in my dreams, and sometimes I would wake terrified, feeling as though I was still his prisoner, that my escape had only been a trick of the mind. Then, slowly, sanity would return.

On the third day, a colleague, Rick, called from work to ask why I had not come in. I stammered something about being sick. Rick commiserated and asked when I could come in. They were having a problem with the computer system.

So the world pulled me back. I spent the next few days working out and fixing the glitch. Having to focus helped me a great deal. When two other technicians took me out for pizza after it was all done, I saw myself in the mirrors that ran along two walls of the restaurant. There I was, a skinny Indian guy with stubble on my chin and pizza sauce at the corners of my mouth, grinning and guzzling like everyone else. Rick's people had emigrated here three generations ago from Holland. Aichiro was a second-generation Japanese immigrant. So what if I'd come from a farther shore than anyone else? This was Boston, one of the great melting pots of the world, where nearly everyone was a stranger. My two colleagues were both married, and I too had someone I loved, someone to wait for. The revelation about my true identity seemed, all of a sudden, irrelevant.

As soon as I could take leave from my job, I booked a flight to India. It was too late to attend Sankaran's wedding. Much as I wanted to see him, I felt this wasn't the right time. As for Janani, I had no idea what I would say to her, but she owed me some answers. I also had to admit to a growing worry about her silence. Why had she not written to me? What had happened to her in Thailand? Surely it could not be a coincidence that she and Moghe had been headed to the same place?

I did not know how much I had missed being in India until I was in Delhi, taking in great lungfuls of warm air that smelled of car exhaust, roasting corn cobs, and eleven million people. From the Interstate Bus Terminus I took a night bus to Rishikesh, traveling with a group of elderly pilgrims who took pity on me and shared their dinner of parathas and pickled mangoes. As dawn came I woke from uneasy slumber to find myself breathing in the scent of the Himalayas.

It took the auto-rickshaw man only about ten minutes to locate the address I gave him. He piloted his little vehicle through narrow, twisting streets, past amiable gatherings of cows, goats, and people to a small row of shops. Their shutters were still down, and the shopkeepers were bustling about in front of their shops, putting up the cots they had slept in. At last I came to the place Janani had lived in for the past ten years.

I searched for her with my mind, but she was not there. A handsome, middle-aged woman in a blue cotton sari was raising the shutters. She was chewing on a neem twig. Every few seconds she would rub her teeth with the twig and spit in a corner in front of the shop. (I remembered, with a pang, Janani teaching me how to brush my teeth in just this manner). Behind the woman I could see two large, old-fashioned sewing machines and a number of finished clothes on racks.

An array of grimy bottles stood on a shelf—Janani's herbal concoctions. I smelled the familiar aroma of tulsi. Heeng. Dried amla.

I put my palms together. "Namaste," I said. "My name is Arun. I am looking for Janani-behn. Are you Rinu Devi?"

Her eyes widened; the neem twig fell from her mouth. Her mind was quivering, tense. I found her reaction puzzling.

"Janani is not here," she said with outward composure. "She has moved to foreign lands."

"I know she went to Thailand," I said, coming into the shop. I was aware of a curious urchin or two hanging about, listening. The woman's mind was bristling with fear and dislike.

"I am just a friend," Rinu Devi said, sounding placating. She gave me a wary look. "Janani's helped me run my shop these past few years. Then recently she met someone and got married and went to Thailand."

She was lying. I looked outside. It was still early, and only a slow car or sleepy bullock-cart went by. The urchins had gone back to their business for the moment.

"Look, Rinu-ji" I said. "I could be nice and spend the next two days trying to persuade you to tell me the truth. Or I could mess with your mind. Janani must have told you what kind of monster I am."

She gave me a look of loathing.

"If you must know, Janani went to a place near Bangkok; I don't remember the name, because she heard that one of your kind had landed there. Someone new. She went to organize a burning. It's been nearly a month and she has not been back. How can I say what happened to her?"

"Did she leave any message, any note?"

"No. She wasn't one to confide in me about these things. She told me just this: that she might not return. She expected danger." Rinu Devi's mind was calmer now. She was feeling more confident. Yet, under the façade I sensed strong emotion.

"That's all she told you? Why didn't she confide in you?"

"She knew I don't like her involvement in the network. I've never understood why she wouldn't just want to kill the aliens instead of…of changing them. We…we had disagreements."

I took a deep breath.

"What network?"

She raised her eyebrows in mock astonishment.

"Oh, she didn't tell you? There are other people like her who can sense the aliens. Whenever they hear of an unusual event—like reports of strange lights in the sky—they go to that place. If they find one of your kind, they burn them to take away their power. What's left is like an empty gourd."

"Where is this network? Where are the other people like me?"

She curled her lip. Her mind trembled with spite.

"Mostly in mental hospitals," she said. "Or wandering the streets, begging, I don't know. Janani didn't go far enough with you—she said you called out to her, as your old self died. She pulled you out of the fire too early."

45

I sensed it then: my ghost self. It stood at the edge of my consciousness, a limb raised, as though to beckon. But I am dead, I thought. I am dead.

Into the silence between us came the sounds of shutters being opened, a cot being dragged across the ground. Mingled with the smell of Janani's herbs was the pungent scent of pine. Away and below us the great Ganga rushed frothing toward the plains.

When I spoke my voice was barely a whisper.

"But why…why do they do this to us?"

I already knew the answer. In her last letter Janani had said that they had to burn me to save me, to make me human. Rahul Moghe had escaped this ordeal by fire, she wrote, and look how dangerous he was. But apart from him, she had said nothing about others like me or about a network. Perhaps my species was indeed hostile to humankind. And yet…what if that was not the case with every individual? What if some of us were different? What right did Janani and her network have to deny us the chance to be who we were?

"You really don't know much, do you?" said Rinu. Her tone had lost some of its bite. "You are alien— enemy. You want to subdue us, enslave us!"

"But—" I began. She waved an impatient hand.

"I can't answer your questions. I don't know who these network people are. I just wanted her to leave the whole thing, to have a life with me…"

Her eyes filled with tears. I sensed her mind turning over, like a cat turns on its back, exposing the belly. Here she was, vulnerable, all pretence lost. Her hatred of me was not gone, but contained, as water is by a dam.

"Did you love her?" I asked.

She wiped her eyes with the free end of her sari.

"How could I not? We were friends as girls." She hesitated, looked at me with defiance, chewing the end of her neem twig with strong white teeth. "We began like sisters, but then we fell in love. She left me to work for the network. When she came back here after years, I thought...I thought..."

"You thought she had come back to you, but she was still working for the network."

She nodded. Eyes that had once been beautiful peered out from a nest of premature wrinkles. Lines of discontent surrounded the well-shaped lips. Her hair was tied in a bun, the free end of the sari draped over her head. Her sari was blue, not white, but I knew I was looking into the face of a mourner.

"So she said nothing about this network," I said at last. "You didn't see her meet anyone..."

"I don't know anything about those people," she said. "Janani knew I would be upset if she talked about them. Always, letters came for her, and phone calls at the booth in the next lane. I don't know anything."

She made space for me on a mat on the floor. Through the one shutter she had opened, pale light came in. She went to the front and yelled to a boy to bring tea.

The tea came in chipped glasses, milky and strong with the scent of cardamom. I sipped and listened to Rinu talk about her life with Janani. She kept rubbing tears away from the corners of her eyes.

"Why are you so certain she is dead?" I asked her. Without a word she got up, went behind a curtain at the back of the shop and returned with an envelope that she handed to me. When I opened it I found a piece of newsprint torn from an English language daily based out of Bangkok. With it was a note in a crude hand that said simply—*Sorry. She was one of our best.* It was signed A.R.

"The man at the tea-shop read it to me," she said, pointing to the newspaper fragment. "I don't read English—not enough."

The news brief said only that there had been an explosion in an abandoned warehouse in a locality on the outskirts of Bangkok. Three people had been killed, two of them women. One of them was believed to have been a tourist from India, one Janani Devi. The heat from the explosion had been so great that nothing recognizable had been left of the bodies. Witnesses had seen the three people entering the warehouse just before the explosion.

I stared at the dirty little piece of paper, numb with grief and anger. This only confirmed what I had feared all along—that Janani was dead. I would never be able to confront her now, never have answers to my questions. Never receive letters from her, full of scolding and advice...

Rinu leaned forward, patted me on the shoulder. She wiped her face with the end of her sari. I thought of Rahul Moghe in the hotel room, the phone call, and his face filled with hunger and anticipation as he said "Bangkok."

Who had called him? Who had told him about the next landing? Had he known Janani would be there?

For that matter, how had he known—twice—where to find me?

"You betrayed her, didn't you?" My words came out brokenly.

Her shapely lower lip trembled. Perhaps she thought I could read her mind. But the pieces were slowly coming together.

"You were the one who told Rahul Moghe I had gone to America. Someone must have been telling him. How else would he find me in San Francisco and Boston? You couldn't read the English return addresses on my letters to Janani, but perhaps you could read enough to make out the city I was in. Tell me, did you phone him from somewhere, or did you write?"

She flinched, then gathered herself together and stood up. I stood up also, trembling with rage. She spat at my feet.

"Yes, yes, I betrayed her. I told Rahul Moghe that she was going to Bangkok, that they had found one of his kind. I knew he would find her and confront her, perhaps kill her. So what! She betrayed our love a hundred times. I always came second for her. Even to you—you!"

Tears slid down her face, and a wave of jealous hatred rose in her mind.

"You! A thing, a creature from another world—she loved you better than me! Serve her right! But I never knew what it would be like without her. I thought I could just go back to the time ten years ago before she returned. I had become free of wanting her, you see…"

My mind lashed out at hers like the talons of a predatory bird. I had never been able to do this before. Suddenly, I knew I could hurt her. I drew back. I looked at her, now sobbing at my feet. A face peered around the shutters.

"Anything wrong, Rinu-behn?"

It was the barber's wife from next door; she glared suspiciously at me.

"It's all right," I said. "It's just some bad news I brought. Death in the family. Look after her—I must be on my way."

I left that miserable creature sobbing in the arms of her neighbor and went away, feeling a hundred curious eyes on me.

In my little hotel room I lay on my bed and stared at the ceiling for what seemed like days. The sun rose and set in the two small windows that faced each other, and each time dark fell, I saw the stars of Sapt-Rishi burning in a velvet sky.

Sapt-Rishi...Sankaran showing me star charts on his computer.

I roused myself, made a phone call to Sankaran's home in Chennai. It would be good to see him, I thought. But he wasn't there. I talked to his mother, who spoke with enthusiasm about the wedding. She told me that Sankaran and his bride had gone to Ootacamund for their honeymoon.

I thought of Sankaran in the blue Nilgiri hills, the stars spreading in the sky above him like a great, sequined quilt. Would he lecture his wife on celestial objects? Would she listen to him as I had? A great wave of envy and loneliness swept over me.

I spent the remaining week of my leave wandering around the hill towns near Rishikesh. I bathed in the holy waters of the Ganga with the other pilgrims. I went to a lonely shrine of Lord Shiva's, high in the mountains. Moved by a strange impulse, I set before the stone lingam a small offering of marigolds. In the little hill towns I walked the crowded streets restlessly, enjoying, despite my grief and loneliness, the anonymity that I had nowhere else in the world.

When I returned to Boston, I was in the lowest of spirits. I had lost everything, including my illusions about myself. Sankaran was my last resort. I needed the healing touch of his mind, the restful pleasure of his company. Meanwhile I wondered uneasily about Rahul Moghe. He seemed to have vanished from my life, but I could never rid myself entirely of his presence. It was as though he had left a splinter lodged in me, a ghost of a voice that called to me with a longing that could not be denied, an endless summons of desire that reminded me of the bull I had seen once on a street in New Delhi.

Sankaran's itinerary was posted on my fridge. As the day of his return approached, I became more and more nervous. What if his wife were a tyrant? What if she restricted his movements so that we could no longer meet? How could I make a claim on him that would be at least equal to that of his wife?

How does a man who is not a man or a woman, not a human or an alien—how does such a being confess his love to another man?

Then it came to me: I would tell him my story.

Not all at once, but with hints and intimations at first.

I shook all over at the thought. With Janani gone, there was nobody in the world excepting Rinu and the network who knew what I was. What better evidence of love and trust could I give Sankaran?

On an impulse I went to the local bookstore and bought the most lavish card I could find. In it I wrote:

> *Dear Sankaran,*
>
> *Lord Shiva has given me an answer to one of the questions you asked him. There is life on other worlds. Let's talk about this.*
>
> *Your Friend,*
>
> *Arun.*

I put the card in an envelope and pushed it under the door of his apartment. Breathlessly I waited for his return, for the time when I could once more sink my mind into the cool stream-bed of his being. On the day that he was to arrive I decided to surprise him by meeting him and his wife at the airport.

Because there was a traffic pile-up on the highway, I was late getting to the airport. When I rushed into the baggage claim area, most of the passengers from his flight had left. I looked around for him for a while. Finally I realized that he must have already gone home.

I drove like a madman to his apartment. When I arrived, I found Sankaran and his wife relaxing over coffee. Sankaran welcomed me and introduced me to his wife.

She was all aglitter in a blue silk sari and gold jewelry. Her eyes were like black beetles. She smiled coldly and disapprovingly at me. With a shock I realized that I could not sense her mind at all. She was a blank.

As for Sankaran, I sensed that the clarity and beauty of his mind was already being undermined by the confusion and contradictions that characterize the ordinary person. There were only hints of damage now, but the clean, clear transparency of his soul that had sustained me was breaking up into bubbles, little patches of opacity. He was dissipating before my eyes.

What had she done to him?

She was holding the card I had put under the door. She wrinkled her nose as though she had picked it up out of the trash and handed it to him.

"What's this?"

He glanced at it without (apparently) noting my untidy scrawl. He shrugged his shoulders, put the card on the desk, and smiled fondly at his wife, following her movements with his eyes as she poured me a cup of coffee. He was already only peripherally aware of me.

My heart clenched in my chest. I drank my coffee in a few gulps, burning my tongue, made my excuses as quickly as I could, and left them to their domestic bliss.

The next time I saw Sankaran, I didn't see him. I was in the café, and he walked in with his wife, and I didn't even feel the quiet, clean wave of his mind wash over and refresh my soul.

I remembered then what physicists say about solitons—eventually they all dissipate.

It is hard for me to recall with composure the days after these events. I lived in a surreal, depressive daze in which night and day blurred into one another. My mind dwelled constantly on death and loss.

When my company folded and I lost my job, I left Boston and began to travel. My depression gave way to the restlessness that had always been a part of me. I moved from port to port, taking up jobs in short spells, staying only as long as the wanderlust let me. I felt as though I was being shadowed—whether it was by my ghost self or Rahul Moghe, I could not tell. A footfall on a quiet street in the outskirts of Atlanta. My hotel door in Milan creaking open, then shut, while I lay half-asleep on the bed. A whisper in a darkened street in Ankara, saying my name. Through this troubled time I continued to experiment with mind-weaving, but without the enthusiasm of my earlier days. I was only too aware that whatever pleasure it gave me was temporary—and that it underlined the fact that I was not human.

Eventually I washed up on Indian shores. It was a relief to be back; I took comfort in the small but immutable fact that I looked like everybody else. I knew the sense of belonging was illusory, but it eased my mind a little.

I took up a job as a lecturer at a college in South Delhi. Something about the slow circumlocutions of the ceiling fans, the languor of heat-stupefied students, the cool rush of air-conditioned air in the computer rooms—took me back to my own days as a young student, when I had not a care in the world and Janani was still part of my life. I used my skills with mind-weaving, crude as they were, to settle disputes, to help students understand each other. This should have given me some satisfaction, but at the end of the day when I went up to my two-room flat, only the familiar despair awaited me. At times I wanted to end my life, but the same inertia that kept me from living also kept me from dying by my own hand.

Then I met Binodini.

Her mind was muscular, strong, beautiful. Its fluxes and transformations were smooth, controlled, like a dancer executing a familiar turn. Although she could not sense my mind exploring hers, I had difficulty manipulating its topography to make a meta-mind with another. There was a discipline about her that, while quite different from the high-Himalayan feel of a soliton's mind, had a similar, if muted effect on me—a subtle quieting, a calming. In appearance she was a middle-aged woman with graying hair that she did up carelessly in a bun; her face was calm, her large, sympathetic eyes observant.

She taught sociology. I had seen her at faculty meetings and liked the shape of her mind; one day, when I was nursing a cup of tea alone at a stained wooden table in the café, she asked if she could join me. It turned out she was a divorced single woman without children. She did research on groups that believed in supernatural phenomena including UFO sightings.

"Do you believe in aliens?" I asked her, hoping I sounded jocular.

She smiled. "There are things I've come across in my research that I can't explain. So I keep an open mind." She looked at me over her cup of chai. "Something tells me that your question wasn't a casual one. Is there an experience you've had that you can't explain either?"

I wasn't ready to tell her, but it occurred to me with an immense sense of relief that perhaps I had found a confidante.

Life wasn't easy for her. She was not interested in a relationship and had to keep fending off men who couldn't understand that. There was a controlled fierceness about her, a courage and curiosity that kept her going. She kept a little vegetable garden behind her apartment, where she grew red radishes and brinjal, and simla mirch. I still recall the color and roundness of freshly uprooted radishes in the blue ceramic bowl on her kitchen table, the crunch of her strong white teeth as she bit into one. She did an hour of yoga every morning.

"I'd be dead without yoga," she told me. "Disciplines the mind."

She gave me a shrewd look.

"It's also good if you're in mourning."

It was then that I told her. That morning—classes had been canceled due to some unrest in the city—

we'd walked off campus together, and she had invited me into her home.

She listened well. I don't think she necessarily believed me the first time, but she didn't disbelieve me either. To my own ears my story sounded ludicrous, but her sympathy was real, without condescension.

One evening I invited her to my apartment for dinner. That was when I showed her what evidence I had for my story: the broken metal and ceramic bits that were presumably the remains of my ship; the photos, Janani's letters. She looked at everything with a scholar's interested gaze, mingled with child-like wonder. When she looked at me her eyes were bright; she hugged me.

"Take me to your leader," I said, to stop my own tears. And we laughed helplessly.

The evening came and went. We talked into the early hours of the morning, sitting at my little dining table over endless cups of tea, like old friends. By then I was filled with a mad euphoria, composed of equal parts of relief and exhaustion.

"So tell me," she said at one point, "which of the thirty-four states am I?"

I stroked my chin, put on a professorial air.

"Dr. Binodini Das, your diagnosis is number thirty-five! A mind such as yours has never been seen before..."

She grinned, punched me lightly on my shoulder.

"No, really, Arun, tell me. I find all this very interesting..."

"I wasn't really joking," I said. "I'm rethinking that concept of the thirty-four genders. I think it's like colors in a spectrum—you can call this red and that orange. but there is no real dividing line between the colors. One bleeds into the other. You feel…mauve to me."

"Mauve," she said thoughtfully, smiling. "Lucky for you I like that color."

After that we spent a lot of time together. We went to movie theaters and watched bad science fiction films. We sat in the café and talked. I sensed that she was holding off on becoming intimate with me, which at first upset me. But I knew that although our friendship had brought a lightness into my heart, the despair was still there. I was still haunted by what had happened to me, and she knew it.

"You know you have to find him, don't you?" she told me after we emerged from a showing of "Antariksh ki Yatra."

The crowd was spilling out of the exit doors; my feet crunched on popcorn. A teenager was shouting into her cell phone; somewhere I smelled henna. A man looked at me from the doorway and smiled, apparently mistaking me for someone else. His face changed when I stared at him.

Outside under the neem trees it was dark, quiet. The earth smelled damp from yesterday's rain. Tonight the stars were partly obscured by city haze and light pollution. As was my habit I looked for the star that was my native sun, but the constellation Sapt-Rishi was lost in the haze.

"Whom do I have to find?" I said, although I knew whom she meant.

"Rahul Moghe."

His name, unspoken for so long, sent an electric shock through me. My ghost self arose in my mind as though it had been waiting for those very syllables. I felt a great wave of fear and longing.

Over the next few days Binodini argued with me, and ultimately I gave in. She was simply repeating to me what my own mind had been trying to tell me: that if I were to have any peace in this life I would have to confront Rahul Moghe, to find the answers to the questions that had plagued me half my life. And then I would have to make a decision.

"All right," I said at last. From pursued, I would become the pursuer. But how would I find him?

"You'll find him," Binodini said confidently.

One day I confessed to her my greatest fear. What if I joined forces with Rahul Moghe and turned against humanity as he had done? "He would kill you without a thought," I told her. "Do you want me to become like that?"

"Listen, Arun, whatever decision you make, you will still be you. Alien or human—those are just words, labels. You are what you are."

So I went looking. Because I didn't know where to find Rahul Moghe, I followed the trails of disasters, riots, unexplained violent events. But all these turned out to be the work of human beings alone. Wherever he was, Rahul Moghe was not trying to attract my attention.

One evening I was in a train returning from one of these trips. The Shatabdi Express was tearing through the night across the Gangetic plain. I was in a second class, air-conditioned compartment; my fellow travelers were asleep, but I was wide awake, leaning against the window, watching my reflection in the glass. The impenetrable night outside made the compartment seem like a cocoon, a world unto itself. Yet, as the train swayed and sang in rhythm, it seemed to be singing his name.

"Rahul Moghe, wherever you are, let me find you," I said in my mind, with all the fervor of my despair.

I didn't know I had also spoken aloud. The man in front of me, huddled in a blanket, stirred; black eyes snapped open. His mind woke suddenly, but he closed his eyes and feigned sleep. There was a suitcase under his bunk, embossed in gold letters: Amit Rajagopal.

It wasn't him. I would have known Rahul Moghe anywhere from his mind's signature. This man's mind seemed vaguely familiar but perhaps it was just that he reminded me of someone at the college. I didn't pay much attention to him because something in my own mind woke up when I made my plea.

How can I describe it?

It's like falling asleep with the radio on very low. The sound does not disturb your sleep or your dreams, except perhaps to give them a certain haunted quality, but when you wake up it is there. So I heard his voice in my mind as it woke, calling to me very faintly across a vast distance.

"I'm coming!" I said, and in that moment there was no fear in my heart.

He would not wait but would meet me half-way. I don't know what means he employed to travel from wherever he was, but early that morning I stepped off the train at a tiny station where this train normally did not stop. He must have arranged it by tinkering with the engine driver's mind. The thought made me shudder. I knew this was the place.

The brick station platform was edged with lush bougainvillea bushes with red flowers. Apart from the blanket-wrapped people asleep on the platform in the early morning stillness and a small band of crows raiding the garbage, there was nobody. In the field by the station, men, young and old, squatted at their ablutions, their water pots agleam in the early sun. They watched the train go by and did their business without embarrassment. I walked through the nearly empty stationhouse where I smelled tea brewing. Lata Mangeshkar was singing a bhajan on the radio. I came out into the narrow lanes of a small town.

He was in a ramshackle hotel room not far from the station. Our minds met as I climbed the stairs. I didn't have to knock; he opened the door and let me in. He was in the same form as when I'd seen him last: a wiry Indian man who seemed larger than he was. The room was dingy, with a dressing table and a tarnished mirror in an ornate brass frame. A single, sagging bed was covered with a blue, patterned sheet, and paan stains showed through the white-washed walls. A calendar with a buxom movie star hung on the wall by the window. I could see the street below, already crowded with bicycles, and a few cars lurching behind them, honking. The air was full of the sounds of bicycle bells.

Rahul Moghe did not touch me but bade me sit on the only chair in the room.

How can I describe that meeting? Here was the being I had feared and loathed for so many years of my life, who had killed innocent people, had done to death the one human being who had loved me and cared for me: Janani. And yet…he was my own kind. Between our minds there were no barriers. With him I could begin to learn the lexicon of my lost language.

I touched his mind tentatively; I could have lost myself exploring its dizzying contours. But when the whole mass shifted and loomed over me like a great blue whale turning, I withdrew in panic.

"I forgot," he said, and his voice startled me in the room. "Last time. You weren't used to how we communicate. I should have given you more time."

The questions and challenges I had for him dried on my tongue. It took me some time to speak. All the while his eyes looked hungrily at me. Leopard's eyes, burning in that gold-brown face.

"I want to know…I need to know more about what I…what we are," I said. "Why we are here. Why you've done what you've done."

"Let me touch you," he said. "Not mind-to-mind, if that frightens you still, but I can't explain things very well by speech alone. I must have contact."

I put my hand on his arm. He shivered, and it seemed to me that his arm would change, that he would change form any moment, but he didn't.

"You don't know how long I searched for you," he said. "I went all over the world… Then it came to me that I would have to wait for you to come home to me. All these years I have been waiting."

I don't know what I had expected of this meeting, but the almost anti-climactic quietness of it was something I had not anticipated.

"Let me tell you about our people," he said. "According to the lore, when our species was still young, yet old enough to go out among the stars, we colonized several worlds, this one among them. Then our own world fell into an age of darkness and ignorance. Instead of letting each other meld and fuse and thereby achieve greater harmony, we put up barriers. We fought. We lost ourselves and our history. You must understand that a species such as ours does not record data on stone—we have no need of it. When we die, we simply rejoin the formless substrate that holds all our memories. New ones are born from that substrate with bits and pieces of the old knowledge. When we meld with another, we recover it for all of ourselves.

"When I was young we had recovered some fragments, enough to know how to build ships again to navigate the seas of the sky. But there had been no contact between us and the colonized worlds for eons. Our history would not be complete until the colonizers came home and mingled with us. So some of us set out. I landed on this planet and began my search for our kind."

I could feel his mind straining to speak its own language, to tell me mind-to-mind what those first years had been like. The escape from the first burning. The destruction of the spaceship. The endless wanderings from continent to continent to find the colonizers. And then, a stupendous discovery.

"The first wave of colonizers had taken over the native species as we have done on our own and other worlds," he said. "It is a form of perspective-borrowing, where you get to see from the point of view of the animal what the universe looks like to it. But the colonizers had gone a step further. They had, in fact, joined with the mind-shapes of the natives—turned native, in a manner of speaking, so that they no longer remembered who they were.

"Have you ever wondered why you found it so easy to get into the minds of the animals here? The humans, more than any other species? It is because at some level the colonizers still remember their old language. Why do you think the average human is such a messy mix of contradictory emotions? Why do you think they feel alienated, not only from each other but from their own selves?"

He fell silent.

"But why do you destroy the humans, then," I asked, "if part of them is like us?"

The mountain ranges of his mind quivered, loomed large over me.

"Why? Why? You can ask that?"

He clutched my hand and pulled me to the bed. His hand burned as though with fever. He put his face close to mine. His eyes were empty sockets in which danced a universe of stars.

After a while he could speak again.

"When I made my discovery I realized I had to free our people, the first colonizers, from their bondage to this species. I could not go home; my spaceship had been destroyed. If another of our kind came to this planet we could return on their ship, or we could put our minds together and send forth a beacon into space, a message calling for help.

"But that woman—that viper—destroyed the few who came. So I realized that there was another way.

"If I could do the right kind of mind-weave between human minds, I could project a message into space, a weak one, but enough that it could be picked up. But for that I need your help. I have not succeeded because I need another to hold the structure. It will be the largest structure ever built, at least a hundred thousand human minds…"

It was like making waves on a string, I realized. You need a person at each end.

"I think," he resumed, "that this great melding of minds will free the original colonizers from their current state. They will realize who they really are. They will leave with us when the ship comes. Even if they cannot take corporeal form, we can find some way to take them with us. To go home…"

His mindscape convulsed when he said the word "home." All these decades he had experienced the utter loneliness of the foreigner whose language nobody knows.

"I haven't melded with a mind for years," he said. "They left enough of you that I could at least get a taste of what it used to be like. You know, among our species, when we mate, nothing is hidden. We know each other as truly as it is possible to know another being. And then, when we have tired of the world and need rest, we sink into formlessness, to rise again as another consciousness.

"How inadequate this language is! Come, now, let me show you in the way that you will truly understand. I cannot tell you what it is like…to actually be there."

We leaned toward each other. I could not help it. I suppose I had made the decision already that I would remain with him, two of a kind, marooned on this world. Perhaps I had hopes of ultimately being able to stop him from wreaking havoc on humankind. I don't know. All I wanted at that moment was to know again what it meant to meet mind-to-mind with my own species.

How can I explain that need? I was trapped in this male, human, unchanging body; only with my mind meeting his could I have the freedom to transcend these boundaries, to soar above the barriers that humans make between each other, and between humankind and all else. To know another being in a way that surpasses ordinary intimacy. My human fears dissipated; my ghost self appeared in my mind, beckoning.

Our attention was on each other, so it startled us both when there was a thunderous knocking at the door and shouting outside. We had already drawn together; the top of his pale yellow shirt was unbuttoned and I could smell, incongruously, cologne on his skin. In that moment as we sprang apart, I saw what hung from his neck on a black thread.

It was a human finger. It looked fresh; somehow the nail gleamed pinkly, which seemed unnatural, because it must have hung on his neck these many years, a trophy. It had once graced Janani's hand. I was sure of that.

"Fire!" shouted the man at the door. He left us and ran to the next door, shouting. Downstairs we could hear more yells, confusion. I smelled smoke.

Rahul Moghe stared fiercely at me.

"Have you led those vipers to me? Is this a betrayal, after all?"

"No!" I said. "Let's get out quickly. I don't know, it may just be an ordinary fire."

But even as I said it I knew that it wasn't so. I had been followed. That man on the train...his initials, A.R. Like the signature on the note that Rinu had showed me, those years ago in the Himalayas.

They must have been keeping track of me for a long time.

The lower part of the building was in flames. Men were leading cattle out from one of the rooms, which had apparently been used as a barn. Bits of straw floated in the smoke. A crowd of passers-by had already collected; some were hauling buckets of water.

Rahul Moghe and I pushed through the crowds. The streets were full of people, bicycles, cattle and noise. Like him, I wanted to find a quiet place where we could be together. The knowledge of what the string around his neck held throbbed in my consciousness.

We found an empty field behind a house that was being constructed. At this time house and field were both deserted. Great piles of red brick lay in rectangular stacks around us. There was some kind of storage shed in the field, with a massive padlock on its wooden door. We stopped in front of it and looked at each other. His mind quivered with hunger. I nodded.

He put his finger into the padlock keyhole, thinning it into the right shape, and the lock clicked open. We went into the darkness of the hut, which was lit only by a narrow slit of a window. Inside were dusty bags of cement. I sensed a rat mind as the creature slithered away between the bags.

What I had seen, what I hadn't told him, was that a man had slipped behind us as we left the crowds outside the hotel. One man, maybe two. The interesting thing was that they were both blanks. I could not sense their minds, nor could Rahul Moghe.

That finger. That is what stopped me from warning him.

I thought to myself: I will pull him out of the fire before they completely destroy his mind. He will be like me, then, a creature with whom I can meld my own mind, but who will no longer be able to destroy humankind. After all, this world isn't so bad; I don't even remember the other one. We'll be marooned together...

He must have sensed some change in my mindscape; I think it was only his need of me that stopped him from probing too deeply. Perhaps he thought only that I was afraid.

"I will be careful with you," he told me, as he reached toward me. I felt myself go under as the great waves of his loneliness and longing washed over me. Then there I was, sailing with him as though on the waves of a vast sea. He was beginning to change shape, very slowly out of consideration for me.

I opened my mouth to speak, to warn him after all, maybe, but he closed it with his own. Limbs emerged from his trunk, embracing my own body, fitting against me like no human ever could, making allowance for the rigidity of my form. How trapped I felt then, in my human, unchangeable body!

Outside, there was a muffled explosion; I saw that the thatched roof over our heads was on fire. The walls of the hut were mud and straw. People—the blanks, I don't know how many there were—were battering the walls down. A flaring torch fell through the slit window.

And still, for a moment, he held me, our minds and bodies locked in the closest embrace I have ever experienced. Then it came to him that we were trapped.

"Help me!" I cried. Part of the roof had fallen in—fortunately not the part directly above our heads—and I could see sky through the smoke. I pulled him to this spot. We opened a bag of cement and threw it on the flames, but still they smoldered around us. Brands of burning wood were being thrown through the gap in the roof. We were choking, coughing. I thought to myself, this is how I will die, with him.

"Change form!" I cried. "Change into a bird—fly away! They are not interested in me. Go!"

"It is too late," he said hoarsely. "Besides, I will not leave you." We were both kneeling on the dirt floor, gasping for breath. He put his arms around me, and again I felt the great, terrible magnificence of his mind. In my arms he changed form, swiftly, dizzily: he was a horned ape, a squat, tree-like monster, a giant, ameboid, tentacled beast. I felt that great mindscape shudder as though a quake was ripping through it; I saw the glory of structure and form coming apart. His face and body changed; in my arms he was human again, but he felt different, rigid, unchangeable. I wanted to pull him out of the fire before his old self died, as Janani had done for me. I called Janani's name through my charred throat, but all around me was a wall of fire.

I saw her then, Janani, her face incongruously suspended in the fire as though she were part of it, her dark brown hands reaching out for me through the ochre flames. The left hand was missing an index finger.

When I came to, I was lying on the floor in a room. Afternoon light poured in. There was a man lying next to me, his breath warm against my neck. My arms hurt; now I saw that they were clasped tightly around the man.

A face hung over me; the person was gently trying to disengage my hands. As he did so, the man I had been holding rolled over on to his back, apparently unconscious.

It was Rahul Moghe in his permanent form. Only he looked exactly like me.

"He imprinted on you," a voice said. I saw that there were other people in the room; the one who was speaking now was my train companion, A.R. He wasn't a blank, but the others were.

"Janani," I croaked. My throat felt burnt. There were tender spots all over my body.

"Where's Janani?"

A.R. frowned. "Janani has been dead for years," he said. "That fellow—Rahul Moghe—killed her. I thought you knew."

"But," I began, then gave up. Someone said "Hush, be still." The man was a doctor; he was leaning over me, applying some kind of ointment. Soothing my burns.

"You suffered smoke inhalation and some pretty bad burns," he said. "But you'll be all right. We dare not take you to a hospital lest questions be asked."

I turned my head, not without pain, to indicate Rahul Moghe. Seeing his face was a shock all over again. I could have been looking into a mirror.

"What about him?"

"He's going to be fine," the doctor said. "He's harmless now."

He was harmless all right. That great mindscape was gone, and in its place...a shadow. Nothing left but a ghost. After all this, I had not saved him; I had not pulled him out in time.

He stirred, opened his eyes. They were as vacant as an idiot child's. A thin line of drool trickled down from one corner of his lips.

"Rahul?" I said, and began to weep.

Later they told me that there must always be a human holding the alien in their grasp when the fire is lit, so that the alien would take up the form of that person. In my own burning the person had been a young friend of Janani's, part of the network. He had later been killed by Rahul Moghe.

"How did you know where I was?" I asked my captors. I think it was the second day of my recovery. I lay on a bed, my body covered with bandages. Rahul Moghe drooped in a chair in a corner, looking at nothing.

"We've been...keeping track of you," said the man called A.R.

A terrible thought occurred to me.

"Not Binodini?"

"Not Binodini," he said, but I could not tell whether he was, with gentle mockery, simply repeating my words, or whether he meant that she had nothing to do with this. Was it a coincidence that she had been the one to persuade me to look for Rahul Moghe? She had connections to groups that kept track of UFO sightings. If she was part of the network, she would know that the only way they would find him would be through me.

I don't know that I'll ever know.

Rahul Moghe is at a special home for the retarded. I go to see him nearly every month. When he sees me, something like recognition comes into his eyes. Sometimes he laughs, sometimes he sets up a terrible keening, like a child in pain. He can speak a few words of Hindi, use the bathroom, brush his teeth, but he cannot read. He likes it when I tell him stories, though. I tell him about other worlds and their wonders, and sometimes it almost seems to me that he is remembering.

I still don't know if Janani is alive. A.R. swore to me that she died at Rahul Moghe's hands all those years ago, but my memory of her face in the fire, her hands with that missing finger, is so vivid that I have trouble believing she is gone. She may think it best to stay out of my life, knowing what she's done, what I've been through. If we meet some day I have no idea what I'll say to her.

I've often thought about what Rahul Moghe told me that fateful morning in the hotel room; that people of our own kind came to live in and become part of human minds. I've read about that curious organelle, the mitochondrion that inhabits cells. It was once an independent entity, a kind of bacterium, but at some point in human evolutionary history it ceased to become an invader and instead became an essential part of something larger. If you could offer a mitochondrion its freedom, would it take it?

Now when I explore the mindscape of a human, I wonder which part is my species, and which was originally human. I wonder if the ancestral memories of my species are buried somewhere in the minds of humans. Perhaps they can access these memories only in their wildest dreams. After all, in dreams you can change form, you can walk among other-worldly wonders. The other thing that occurs to me is that while humans (unlike other animals) cannot normally communicate mind-to-mind, that ability might still be latent. So, for instance, some people can tell that they are being watched, or that there is someone besides them in an apparently empty room. Perhaps these are vestigial remains of the original ability to sense and meld with other minds.

After I recovered physically, I went back to my college in Delhi, although my heart wasn't in it. I needed to earn a living so that I could make sure Rahul Moghe was well taken care of. As for Binodini, I have not yet asked her if she betrayed me. I can sense the contours of her mind, but I cannot tell whether she would lie to me or not—her mind is disciplined enough that she might successfully conceal an untruth. Besides, if I don't ask her, I can still persuade myself, sometimes, that she is innocent.

When I returned she immediately understood that I had been through an ordeal; my still-healing body was proof enough. But she knew also that my mind and heart were broken, and she did not press me with questions. I told her only that I had met Rahul Moghe and that he was no longer a danger to humanity. Perhaps she supposed that I had made my choice and that it had been a difficult one. Perhaps she guessed that the possibility of her betrayal might always stand between us. But we no longer met as often as we used to.

I saw my old friend Sankaran again, some time after my return. He came to Delhi University to deliver a lecture. He is now a well-known cosmologist at an institute in Chennai, but he recognized me at once and greeted me affectionately. His wife seemed a lot more relaxed; she chatted pleasantly with me and introduced their seven-year-old daughter, a shy child with a mind as clear and still as lake water with the most interesting undercurrents. All three of them seemed happy, and despite the pain old memories brought me, I was happy for them.

He was no longer a soliton, of course. But that old curiosity, that child-like openness to the marvels of the universe remained, as did his complete lack of pretension. He still apologized to potted plants when he bumped into them. My eyes filled with tears when I saw this; I blinked them rapidly away and laughed with him.

Perhaps the shadow of my old love was still there. We parted with promises of keeping in touch.

One evening Binodini came to my little flat. I was just seeing off some students I had been tutoring; they gave me good natured "aha" glances when she came up the stairs. She had been worrying about my depression, she said. There was a movie in the local theater, a particularly silly science fiction movie we had not yet seen, and would I go with her to see it? I did not want to go, but I let myself be persuaded. In the hot and stuffy theater I sat stiffly in my seat as the drama revealed itself; it was all about aliens on Earth trying to pretend to be human and failing hilariously. Another time it would have sent me into hysterical fits of laughter, but this time I simply felt the sadness come upon me like a wave. Binodini seemed to sense that the movie was not the right one; she pressed my hand as if in apology, and when I stood up to go out, bumping against people's knees and apologizing, she followed.

It was a clear night. The neighborhood next to the theater was suffering a power failure, common in the summer months, so the stars stood out more brightly than they normally did. I looked up at the speck that was my native sun, unfathomably far away.

Binodini took my hand.

I thought of human beings, how they could be, simultaneously, friend and betrayer. Murderer, mother, lover. I, too, had loved and betrayed my own kind.

"You're not alone," Binodini said. "At least, not any more than anyone else."

In that place where we paused, the neon lights of the theater and the sounds of traffic and people were both muted. Under the neem trees the night was thick, so that the candles in the windows of the darkened houses appeared like flickering stars. I could, with a little imagination, see us as adrift in the ocean of space. Home was just a short flight away.

As we gazed up a meteor seared a path through the black velvet sky and disappeared. A meteor, or a ship.

"Wish a wish, Arun!" Binodini said. Her voice was full of tears.

Her hand was warm in mine. She disengaged it gently, and we walked home together through the star-filled night.

About the Author

Vandana Singh was born and raised in India. She was brought up on a diet of myths, legends and other fantastical tales in two languages, Hindi and English. As a teenager she acquired a lifelong interest in environmental and women's issues, and a keen passion for science. She has a PhD in theoretical particle physics and currently lives near Boston with her husband, daughter, and dog. She divides her energies between worrying about global warming, teaching college physics, writing science fiction and fantasy, and spending time with her family. Her short stories have appeared in such anthologies and magazines as *Polyphony*, *So Long Been Dreaming*, *Interfictions*, *The Third Alternative*, and *Strange Horizons*, and have been short-listed for the BSFA and Parallax awards. She is the author of the ALA Notable book for children, *Younguncle Comes to Town* (Viking 2006). A collection of her short fiction, *The Woman Who Thought She Was a Planet and Other Stories*, will come out from Zubaan, New Delhi, in December 2007.

For more about her, please visit her website at http://users.rcn.com/singhvan.

Vandana is indebted to Anita, Ashok, Christopher, and Ramaa for very useful feedback on this story.